I am
Thankful

There is no school today.
Hooray!

I am thankful that
I can stay in bed.

2

Pops wakes me up anyway.
We have a lot to do.
I am thankful Pops lives with us.

Today is Thanksgiving!
First, we help Mom make pies.

Pops chops apples.
I peel sweet potatoes.

Sweet potato pie
is my favorite.

Next, we head to the firehouse.
Dad has to work today.

I am thankful for what
my dad and his crew do to keep us safe.

We help the firefighters.
I peel more potatoes.

Soon it is time for our town's turkey trot.
Some people walk. Some people run.
We all have fun.

I zoom by Pops.
He cheers for everyone.

It starts to drizzle.
I slip on some wet leaves
and fall.

Another runner
helps me.
We finish
the race.

I am thankful for
my new friend.
Pops and I head home.

My cousins are here!
The whole family
will play football
after we eat.
We do this every year.

For now,
we kids practice.

Oh no!
It starts to pour.

We go inside.
We watch football and play games.
It is cozy and warm.

More family arrives.

It gets very loud and a little crowded.

I check on Great-Gran.
She sits in her chair
by the window.
She likes the quiet.

Great-Gran points outside.
The leaves go round and round.
They dance in the wind.

She always spots
something special.

I am so thankful
for Great-Gran.

It is time to eat.
Everyone takes a seat
at the table.

We settle down.

We are thankful
for the tasty food.

We are thankful
for everyone
at the table.

And **we are thankful**
for loved ones
who are not with us.

After dinner,
we all help clean up.

At last, Dad is home!
He has great news.

The rain has stopped.
The wind dried the grass.
The sun is out.

We play football.

But we take a time-out
to eat some pie, too.
Yum!

I am so thankful!

What are **YOU** thankful for?

Can you think of three examples?